Chubby puppies™

Summer Picnic

by Olivia Barham

SCHOLASTIC INC.

New York Toronto London Auckland Sydney
Mexico City New Delhi Hong Kong Buenos Aires

For my daughter, Oriana

No part of this publication may be reproduced in whole or in part, or stored in a retrieval system, or transmitted in any form or by any means, electronic, mechanical, photocopying, recording, or otherwise, without written permission of the publisher. For information regarding permission, write to Scholastic Inc., Attention: Permissions Department, 557 Broadway, New York, NY 10012.

ISBN 0-439-35586-9

License arranged by Equity Marketing, Inc. TM 2002 Morrison Entertainment Group, Inc. Copyright © 2002 Michael Bowling Enterprises #1. All rights reserved. Published by Scholastic Inc. SCHOLASTIC and associated logos are trademarks and/or registered trademarks of Scholastic Inc.

12 11 10 9 8 7 6 5 4 3 2 1   2 3 4 5 6/0

Printed in the U.S.A.
First Scholastic printing, April 2002

Written by Olivia Barham
Illustrated by Karol Kominski
Book Design by Bethany Dixon

Brittany always liked to look her best. Today she was at
the beauty parlor having her fur trimmed and her nails painted
for the summer picnic.

Sophie and the other Chubbies passed by the salon on their way to the park.

"Come on, Brittany," called Sophie. "You're going to be late."

Brittany tied a pink bow in her curls and took a long admiring look at herself in the mirror.

Yes, she thought. *I look very beautiful indeed.*

The Chubbies hurried along on their way to the park.
All except Brittany, who walked slowly, being careful not to
chip her freshly painted toenails on the pavement.

When they got to the park, Peaches laid the blanket down on the grass. Maggie and Scarlet unpacked the picnic basket and set out the cups and plates.

"Over here, Brittany!" called Max. "Come sit down on the grass with us."

"No, thank you," replied Brittany as she fastened her parasol to the back of her chair. "I don't want to wrinkle my new dress."

9

Sophie put ten cherries on each plate. Max cut the watermelon into large triangle-shaped pieces. It was deliciously sweet and juicy.

"This is the best picnic ever," said Peaches.

"Here, Brittany," said Scarlet, offering her a large slice of watermelon. "Would you like something to eat?"

"No, thank you," said Brittany. "The juice might drip on my clean fur."

"Brittany isn't being much fun today," said Sophie. "She is so worried about how she looks."

"Maybe she'll join in when she sees us playing games," said Peaches. "What are we going to play, Max?"

Max was the best at thinking up games. He looked at the plates and the cherry pits. He looked at the plastic forks and cups and the left-over fruit.

"I know," he said. "Let's play Throw the Cherry Pits in the Cup."

Max placed one of the plastic cups on the blanket.
The Chubbies took turns throwing their cherry pits into it.

Sophie was an excellent shot. She got all of her
pits in on the first try!
Peaches took a plate of cherries over to Brittany.

"Here, Brittany," said Peaches. "Why don't you eat some cherries, then you can join in the game?"

"No, thank you," said Brittany. "The cherries will make my paws sticky. I'll just watch, if you don't mind."

Meanwhile, Max was busy inventing another game. He took two plastic forks and pushed them into the ground a few feet away from the blanket.

"The object of the game," said Max, "is to roll your orange between the two forks. The one who rolls the orange farthest and gets it through the forks is the winner."

Scarlet lay down on the grass and carefully got her orange ready to roll. Sophie walked over to Brittany.

"Please come and play with us," begged Sophie. "You must be lonely sitting here all by yourself."

"No, thank you," said Brittany. "I might break one of my nails. I'm fine by myself. Really."

Sophie returned to the others. Max threw a paper plate over to Maggie. It soared through the air.

"Catch, Maggie!" he called. "Come on, Brittany. Come and play with us!"

But Brittany just shook her head.

"I wish Brittany would play with us," said Sophie sadly.
"I guess she doesn't feel like it," said Max. "Maybe she's having fun in her own way."

But Brittany was not having fun. She wanted to join in the games, but she knew that running around would make her hot. Her fur might get dirty. Her bow would probably fall off, and then she wouldn't look her best. And Brittany always liked to look her best.

Just then, the paper plate soared over Brittany's head . . .
and landed right in the middle of the pond.

"Oh, no! How will we get it?" exclaimed Peaches. "None of us knows how to swim."

"Brittany can swim," said Scarlet. "She took lessons last year."

But everyone knew that Brittany wouldn't go near the pond.
They would have to figure out another way to get the plate.

"Look!" said Sophie. "A boat. If the plate won't come to us, we will go to the plate."

Everyone climbed aboard, and Peaches rowed out into the middle of the pond.

Maggie leaned out over the water.
"There it is!" she said, pointing to the plate. Max, Sophie, Scarlet, and Peaches leaned over to get a better look, and . . .

SPLASH! Everyone fell into the water and the little boat turned upside down.

"Help! Help!" they cried. "We can't swim!"

Brittany heard their cries and didn't stop to think. She forgot all about her clean fur, her painted nails, her pretty dress, and her new bow, and jumped quickly into the water.

One by one, Brittany brought her friends safely to the shore.

The Chubbies huddled together under the picnic blanket to dry off.

"You look the best you've looked all day, Brittany!" said Scarlet.

"I do?" said Brittany, looking down at her matted fur and muddy dress.

"Yes, you do," said Scarlet. "You look your best because you're smiling."

"I guess I forgot that having fun and helping my friends is more important than looking perfect," said Brittany. "Can we come back to the park tomorrow? I will eat watermelon, play games, get very dirty, and give you all a swimming lesson."

"Yes!" the Chubbies cheered. "Hooray!"